Grace

By TL Bliss

PROLOGUE

I had been asked by a neighbor's daughter if she could do an interview with me for a school project. She was trying to bring her grades up in English class and one of the ways she could do this was to interview someone and put their words into a story. I agreed to do the interview and we had scheduled a Saturday morning to begin.

The neighbor's daughter, Sarah, was still in school. She loved listening to my stories. Sarah was never fortunate enough to sit on her grandma's lap and hear about her grandma's life. Both of Sarah's grandparents had already passed before she was born and Sarah never had a chance to meet either of them.

I had baked some fresh cookies for Sarah's Saturday visit. She loved my homemade peanut butter cookies. I suppose you could say that I was filling the empty shoes left by Sarah's grandma, in Sarah's eyes anyway. She considered me to be her best friend and I think it was because I spent quality time with her. Coming from a large family, there was generally never enough time to listen to how everyone's day had been, especially with the younger children. Before we knew it, "our Saturday" as Sarah called it had arrived.

She came bustling through the door ready to tackle her mission head-on. She had prepared a list of questions and brought a small tape recorder with her. I never really figured she could be as prepared for what she was going to learn about me, but she most certainly came with the equipment to capture my past and put it on paper for all the world to see.

Thus began our Saturday story …

Chapter One

Sarah was sitting in school tapping her pencil on her desk when her English teacher, Mrs. Bennett, ever so politely asked, "Sarah, are you able to do any extra credit activity to help bring your grade up in English? We need to find a way to help you get at least a B in this class or college will be out of the question for you. I want to do everything I can to help you through this, but you will have to help do a little extra to get there too." Sarah stopped tapping her pencil and looked up at me as if to say, "*brilliant idea*" genius.

"I believe we can get you started on doing some extra writing to bring your grade up, since you like to write."

Sarah glanced up at me again and nodded her head. Without uttering a word, she listened intently to what I was saying.

"I would like to see what you can do in the form of interviewing someone and compiling the work into something we can read and understand. A biography of sorts, I suppose you could call it. Written on someone you are familiar with, but want to learn more about; like a grandparent for instance, or another relative. Does that make sense to you? Are you able to do something like that to help bring your grade up?"

As Sarah nodded her head in agreement, she smiled ear-to-ear as if I had handed her a golden ticket to the college of her dreams.

"I have a list of interview questions if you think you need one, or you are welcome to come up with your own," stated Mrs. Bennett as she flipped and fumbled through papers looking for the list. "Please get this in to me by the end of the school year and make sure it is top notch Sarah. I want to see you signing up for college after graduation."

Sarah stood up from her seat and stated to me that she would try her hardest and wouldn't let me down.

*****

Sarah was a tall, thin young woman. She was mature for her age and walked with a purpose. She knew what she wanted out of life and she was aiming for her goal of becoming a writer. She could sit and write for hours at a time, about anything and everything.

Sarah spent most of her time writing poems and short stories about her own life events. Her favorite story was about helping a couple at a local store. They didn't have enough money to pay for their bread and milk, and Sarah took the money she had saved to buy a new CD and gave it to them. She would read that story over and over when she felt like the world was closing in on her.

Being in high school was tough for a girl. Sarah didn't fit in with the other girls who were flirting with the guys on the football team or shopping every day of the week. She preferred to stay by herself and enjoy the peace and quiet.

Writing was what she wanted to do and she was good at it. She wrote for the school paper and helped some of her friends with English assignments. Sarah's biggest problem was not following the rules all the time. She was the sort of person who followed her own rules and did what she wanted to do.

Sarah was very intelligent, but stubborn too. She knew that she was going to succeed in life, but often wondered who was going to be able to keep up with her. She was not the least bit shy about strutting her "*knowledge stuff*" as she called it.

School was easy for Sarah, maybe even too easy. Her grades struggled due to her inability to get papers turned in on time; not that they weren't great papers, but they were almost always late. Sarah risked her grades all through school because of her temperament. Her renegade nature almost had her expelled due to failing gym class. Sarah absolutely despised gym class and being there. She resented the fact that she was forced to participate in something she hated so much.

*****

Sarah's mother was home folding laundry when Sarah came home from school. It seemed as if her mother was always doing something besides greeting each kid as they walked through the door. She was always too busy with 'other things" to even notice half the time if they had all made it back home safely from school.

Dinnertime was the tell all, heading counting, time of day for Sarah's parents. They would set the table and everyone would sit and bow their heads in prayer before eating. The casual glance at each child and making eye contact was often the only form of communication Sarah had with her mom and dad.

Sarah had longed for the day when she could be the center of even just a little bit of attention from her parents. She knew she loved them despite feeling left out. She knew they loved her too. The family was struggling with their own ways of surviving and Sarah could do little more than take part in the daily ritual of eye contact as her way of saying "*I love you*" to each one of her brothers, sisters, mom, and dad without actually articulating the words.

The family was tight-knit, but in other ways. The older siblings helped the younger kids with homework, getting dressed, packing lunches, putting away clothes, cleaning up, and every day normal things. The younger kids worked on reciprocating what they learned onto the ones even younger than they were. Both parents worked and there still never seemed to be enough money to go around. Sarah's dad worked during the day at the local factory and her mother worked nights at the hospital.

There always seemed to be a constant financial struggle to the everyday life of her parents. Her father always seemed to be tired from working long hours. Her mother was exhausted just as much as her father was after working all night and taking care of the household during the day.

Sarah was able to read between the lines even at her age and knew that she had to find a way to live out her dream of being a writer. She wanted to have a best-selling story that the world loved and could relate to. A movie deal would be the icing on the cake for her, but that was a dream for another day. She had to focus on the here and now before she could jump into the what-ifs.

*****

Sarah saw this task of writing the interview as her way of being noticed in the eyes of those she wanted to see *her*.

She was going to work very hard at becoming the person she knew she could be and it was all going to stem from this interview. She had to make a lasting impression in order to be seen by the echelons that would either make or break her writing career.

Her time had finally come to get a jumpstart on her writing and she was jumping in with all she had. She was bound to make an impression where it needed to be made.

*****

Sarah came over that evening to ask if she could interview me. I wondered why *me* of all people, but was honored that she considered me.

Sarah knocked on the door before she came in. She never waited for a "*come in*" just generally knocked and then entered. I could always tell when she had arrived by her eager way of making herself welcome.

Sarah came into the kitchen where I was setting at the table drinking a cup of hot tea and reading a book. She had a smile on her face, which was different for her. She seemed upbeat and almost demanded my attention, but in a silent way. I sat my book down and asked, "Is there something you want to ask me? Why the smile and hyper-jittery-walking on top of the world appearance?"

As Sarah fumbled through her book bag looking for the newest piece she had written for me to read, she pulled a chair out and sat down. Still not saying a word, she just looked all glowy-like. I knew she had news she wanted to share with me, but I also knew how she had her own rules and would eventually tell me, but on her own time.

*****

"Grace, I need to ask you a big favor." She poured herself a cup of hot water while browsing around the cupboard looking for a tea bag to put in it.

"I need to interview someone and put what they say into something readable. I have to make a story out of the information I gather from the interview." Finding the tea bags, Sarah pulled out a couple and sat them on the table.

"I would like to interview you Grace. I know that you will probably not let me, but I wanted to ask you first. I really need to bring my grade up in English and Mrs. Bennett said that if I interview someone and write what they say into something readable, then she would work on giving me extra credit towards my final grade."

Retrieving her book bag again, Sarah pulled out a list of questions and added a few more to it before looking back up. "Grace, can you help me out and let me interview you?"

I placed the book I was reading down on the table and looked over at her face. She was beaming with excitement and I could still sense some hesitancy in her voice. I stood up to get another hot cup of water for tea, when I saw the tea bag setting on the table for me already. Sarah knew me like a book already. Why in the world would she want to interview someone like me? She could have asked anyone, but she asked *me*.

"Sarah, I understand that you need to work on getting your grades up in school, but shouldn't you focus more on the reason why your grades are down to begin with?" I pulled my chair out to set back down at the table and glanced over to see Sarah's head hanging down; she almost looked ashamed of herself.

"I would be honored to let you interview me, but you have to promise me that you will work on your people skills and stop being so darn stubborn. Do we have a deal?" I extended my hand out to her.

Sarah grabbed my hand with both of hers and shook them. "I understand and will work on playing nicer with others; thanks for letting me interview you Grace." The smile returned to Sarah's face and the gleam came back to her eyes.

"When can we start? I am ready as soon as you are."

"I am not busy at all this Saturday, are you free then?"

Sarah grabbed her book from her bag and skimmed through the dates. She looked up at me with a smile on her face and said; "I have all day Saturday free."

"Good, then we can start this Saturday. Now make sure your mom doesn't need your help with anything and tell her you will be over here so she doesn't worry. Oh and Sarah, make sure your homework is done before you come over; this is for extra credit remember."

Sarah nodded her head and started working on her homework while she sat there drinking hot tea in the peace and quiet.

*****

The day had finally come for Sarah to start her interview; it was Saturday. Grabbing the tape recorder from her desk, Sarah double-checked that her homework was done, and ran downstairs. She found her mother out back hanging up clothes on the line. "Mom, I am going to Grace's house to start the interview with her. I will be back later."

Sarah made eye contact with her mom so she knew that the lines of communication were there. Sarah's mom waved her hand, nodded her head, and stated, "Have a good time Sarah." Sarah grinned and nodded back, closed the door, and headed towards Grace's house.

Sarah was very excited to spend the day with Grace. She had been looking forward to this day to come so she could find out some fascinating facts about her best friend. She rummaged through her back pack making sure she had everything she needed, without missing a step, and still in stride headed towards Grace's house.

Sarah jumped up the few extra steps leading to Grace's door; stepping on all of them would require too much time and she was way too busy to be wasting her valuable time making sure she stepped on each one.

I heard the knock at the door and it opened with the glowing presence of Sarah. I knew it was her since she did not wait for me to answer her knock. I was still in the kitchen preparing for our day when she came bouncing in with her recorder in her hand and a tablet of paper and pencil in the other hand.

"I made it just like I said I would Grace. Ooohhh, look you made me peanut butter cookies! My favorite!" Sarah looked up at me and politely asked if she could have one and I handed her two with a napkin. The tea kettle whistle started howling and the addition of hot tea was added to the cookie.

"Ok Sarah. I am ready for your interview. Did you remember to bring your list of questions?" Sarah had the list neatly folded inside her tablet of paper so she wouldn't forget them. The top of the list had the words "*Saturday Story*" written across the top. What an appropriate name for the day's events I thought to myself. I sat nestled in my seat awaiting my interview.

Chapter Two

Sarah made sure she had extra batteries with her and extra cassette tapes to record the interview she was about to begin. She had previously placed these items in her back pack, but was double checking to make sure they were all still there before she began.

Once everything was where it needed to be, Sarah began by saying, "First, thank you for letting me interview you Grace. I appreciate you letting me take your time on a weekend to work on my grades for school. Second, there are some questions here that you may not want to talk about and that's ok, but I will need to write something down for an answer. I hope you understand."

She glanced at me with a gleam in her eye and I knew she was sincere. I wondered what she would need to ask me about that I might not want to answer as she stated. Sarah knew everything about me for the most part and what she didn't know was something she would never ask about anyway.

Sarah started her interview and she said, "ok, the first question is…Can you tell me your name, what year you were born, and what the main topics of news or what the headlines were at the time?"

"Well, I was born in the summer of 1969. Of course we all know that was the era of the flower children, Woodstock, and hippies." I chuckled when I recalled the days of my earlier youth as I spoke about them.

"I was born in Fayetteville, North Carolina, to a young couple. My father was in the military at the time and my mother was a housewife. Of course, back then women didn't work and the men were either in the military or worked someplace to support their family. My mother was a person of few words to anyone except my father. She would talk to him for hours, but not so much with her children. I guess you could say I never really knew my mother when I was young. Although, I did know who she was; I did not know her on a personal level. Of course, not like kids today who know everything about their parents and family situations."

Sarah's eyes glazed over and a hint of sadness lingered in the air. I knew she was one of the kids I was referring to in my statement. The poor girl knew way more than she should at her age; no wonder life was a struggle for her.

I continued on with my recollection of the past; "Nixon was President back then, but I only remember Ford being in office and very, very briefly at that. I also remember President Carter and Reagan, my goodness that was a long time ago too." I took a moment to reflect on my memories and tried to recall something good to talk about from my childhood. The longer I contemplated my past the more I realized that the "good" memories didn't seem to exist.

*****

Sarah looked up at me with sadness in her eyes and said, "Grace, your childhood was really no different than mine is now. You spent the majority of your time alone, doing your own thing, and never really cared what others thought or even what they were doing."

There was a lot to be said for people who spent a lot of time by themselves. Sarah knew what it felt like to be alone; even in a roomful of people. She knew her outlet was writing, but wondered what Grace did to release all of her pent up anguish from the years she spent alone. Sarah wondered if there was a way that information could be pulled out of Grace through this interview.

While Grace was off to retrieve a box she had stored upstairs in her closet, Sarah made note to dig deeper into the person she knew was hiding behind Grace's eyes. Sarah knew that there had to be a way for Grace to get what was inside out so that it didn't build up and start tearing her apart.

*****

"Well, here it is. This little box holds the secret to my entire past." Grace slid a shoebox over to Sarah who opened it and saw dozens of little pieces of paper, all with something written down on it or a sketched out doodle of some sort.

Sarah was looking through the box and saw a handful of poems that were handwritten tucked at the very bottom of the box. She dug to the bottom, pulled each one out, and opened it up.

"Those are poems I wrote throughout my life. Each has its own meaning in one way or another. Some are as recent as last year. I had to be able to get some of those feelings out, so I wrote poetry." Grace glanced toward the floor as if she were hiding her feelings and didn't want Sarah to see the tears welling in her eyes.

"There are poems in there I had written for my late husband, before he passed. There are poems in there for the children who were killed in Newtown, Connecticut, on December 14, 2012, the Sandy Hook shooting at the elementary school. There is a poem or two in there for the terror attacks on the World Trade Centers on September 11, 2001. There is a poem or two in there for my brother who committed suicide; God rest his soul."

Sarah looked over toward Grace and she had tears rolling down her cheeks. Grace reached over and hugged her gently and said, "There, there; no reason to cry Sarah. Those are just a few poems I wrote when I needed to vent my feelings."

I reached for the poem Sarah had been reading. I wanted to see which one brought the tears to her eyes. I briefly recalled writing the poem titled, "*I Struggle With The Words To Say To You*"; I was at a time in my life where I needed to have comfort and could only find it in prayer.

I wrote this poem to help me come back to reality and realize that I am not the only one who was struggling to live alone and feared the future by myself. Was Sarah able to feel what I was feeling when she read the poem? There was no reason for her to cry unless she was able to understand why it was written, but maybe she is stronger than I realized too. As I sat there reading the poem again, I realized that it was very appropriate even to this very day.

I Struggle With The Words To Say To You

Walking in the path of Jesus
Loving life a little more each day
Battling the demons inside me
Trying to wash my sins away

I struggle with the words to say to you
As I kneel in prayer once more
Wishing you could look deep inside me
Counting each tear that hits the floor

Knowing you died for my sins
Gives me hope to fight another day
Wrapping myself in your words
Oh heavenly father hear me pray

The words are trapped in my heart
Their meaning a twisted mess
Listen to the words I say to you
My captive soul wants to confess

Tighter and tighter I cling to you
Holding onto your prayer
Wishing I could walk closer to you
Feeling your love and knowing you care

The days and nights grow shorter for me
Your words are more like song
Confessing my sins to you each day
Knowing your love will keep me strong

I struggle with the words to say to you
As I kneel in prayer once more
Wishing you could look deep inside me
Counting each tear that hits the floor

Knowing you died for my sins
Gives me hope to fight another day
Wrapping myself in your words
Oh heavenly father hear me pray

I considered Sarah a lot younger than maybe her mind, but it was obvious that this poem had struck a chord with her, as she reached for another poem to read, when I had taken this one from her. Maybe I needed to learn not to be so quick to judge this younger generation of kids; they were obviously not what kids were like when I was her age. Kids these days were made of something more, but I wasn't quite sure what it was.

*****

The shoebox was loaded with Grace's past, written on tiny pieces of paper. I knew there had to be a way for her to get what was bottled up inside of her out; I guess I can cross that much off my list of things to ask her.

"Grace, all of these poems are so good. Why didn't you ever have them published anywhere?" I was in serious need of some fresh air, but didn't have the heart to walk away now. I needed to keep reading what Grace had written down throughout her life. Her feelings were displayed in words and I was putting together her life's puzzle one piece at a time.

The words were not being spoken aloud, but were being *read* from her past. This was a new concept for me since I was not ever in a situation quite like this. I had to figure out how to build a story from these pieces of paper and make it worth the life it had come from. This was about Grace, my best friend; the only person who really "*got me*" and I had to do my best.

As I perused through the papers, my interest was piqued by the way she had written herself little notes about her past. Was she keeping this for when her memory was starting to fade and she wanted to relive her past? Was this her diary in tiny little pieces? Were these poems her way of leaving something more for whoever found them? It was as if she wanted me to put her puzzle together for her. Why else was she sharing these personal stories with me? I was here to do an interview and she was giving me everything she had, both inside and out.

She shared her memories in a subtle calming way while we read the poems she had placed so neatly in the bottom of the box. She was so elegant in the way the box was sorted. The little pieces had notes jotted on them, names and dates, birthdates, anniversaries, timeline information jotted down to forever hold onto. There were newspaper clippings with stories like the attacks of September 11, 2001 folded inside her poem, "*The American Way*" which was her tribute to the fateful event that took place.

She so patriotically spoke highly of the Americans and their fight to become one when the nation was being torn apart at the hands of people who were trying to destroy the American way.

The foreigners who thought they could tear apart something as strong as the American Way were obviously mislead when Shock and Awe brought terror to their world, like they brought to ours.

The American Way

Terror is upon us
Striking at our core
Tearing down our buildings
America is at war.

Lives have been taken too soon
Americans are mourning
Fear and hate pour from us now
Take heed this is a warning.

Causing harm to our people
Spreading fear across this great land
Making Americans rage with anger
Bringing a great nation to a stand.

Americans will overcome this
And proceed on with their lives
Helping out our neighbors
Fathers, children, and wives.

The eagle's wings have spread
The battle has begun
America will not back down
until the war is won.

Cast no doubt, shame, or fear
Americans will dominate
We bring hope to our land
Shedding death and hate.

This great nation protects its own
Do not doubts it core
We become one when called upon
Working together for something more

We protect each other
We strive to become free
Set your spirit fighting and
Be brought back upon your knee.

Keep the American flag flying
High and bright each day
Help your friends and neighbors
That is the American way.

I was delighted reading her written words of comfort, uniting a country that was in shambles. People helping their neighbors and fighting back the best way they could, by not showing fear. Every American flag flying high in support of our mother country who so desperately needed her family.

*****

Sarah was reading the poems and it had become obvious that she was interested in something more than doing just an interview. She was jotting down notes and didn't leave one piece of paper from the shoebox untouched or word unread. I found it invigorating that she even wanted to read my memories tucked away in that box.

As Sarah kept reading, it had dawned on me that she was making notes to help find a way to get my poetry published. Was I ready for that to happen? Did I want the world reading my memories? I had to take some time to think about that before just agreeing to allow her to show the world my shoebox full of things I had stored away, and no one knew about until now; well, my husband knew, but then again he knew everything about me.

I recalled writing the poem for him, "*Hanging Onto Memories*"; how I felt the day the news rang of the shootings in Richmond, Virginia, at the Polytechnic Institute in April 2007. My Mel worked at a college and I feared for his safety every day that he went to work.

I knew that society had been laced with mentally ill people since the budget cuts removed any support for them to get the help they needed. The times were such that anyone could buy a gun and go on a rampage shooting innocent strangers just out of pure lack of respect and the need for medical support for their ailments.

The government had taken away the medical treatment and potential future of the people who were terrorizing perfect strangers, friends, relatives, neighbors, co-workers, or whoever else they deemed necessary by taking their life with a gun.

No one was spared from the terror, no one was saved from the fear of the unknown, and clearly no one was willing to realize what was required to help aid in fixing the problem. Greed is an awful thing when it sets in and it had set in by cutting back on the financial responsibility of taking care of mentally ill people.

How scary had the world become to live in fear of your neighbor when the Bible states very plainly that you are to help your neighbors. How were we to help them? How were we to know who needed the help? How were we to protect ourselves from the slayers when we didn't have an idea of who our neighbors even were. Society had taken that right from us.

Hanging Onto Memories
I wake with you smiling down on me
I try to find your light
I whisper for you peacefully
In the still and empty night

The way you wrapped your arms around me
comforting me with your smile
I miss you more than ever
Wishing you could have stayed a while

Hanging onto memories
Oh the pictures in my mind
Bringing me back to yesterday
A better place, a better time

Your smile was uplifting
Your voice a pleasant song
Missing you right now
Knowing it won't be for long

Seeing your eyes light up
In the photo by the bed
Fills my heart with joy
Feeling your love once again

My days and nights are lonely
Wishing you were here with me
If only life had a better plan
And didn't take you from me

Hanging onto memories
Oh the pictures in my mind
Bringing me back to yesterday
A better place, a better time

Your smile was uplifting
Your voice a pleasant song
Missing you right now
Knowing it won't be for long

My tribute to my husband was written as if he had been taken from me too soon by someone who lacked the ability to know right from wrong.

It was very difficult to put onto paper the words that I would eventually have to speak to him one day. I cried for days after writing that poem. I tried not to show how afraid I was of him going to work and facing the chance of losing his life in such a manner.

As I read the words I had written so long ago to the love of my life, I could not control the tears that had welled up in my eyes and spilled over to run so softly down my cheek.

*****

I never figured that I would be in a position to see my friend shed tears. Grace had been reading through her poems and every now and then would cry. It broke my heart to see her reliving the past in such a way that it broke her heart.

She took the time to reflect on why she wrote the poems and how they were affecting her now. It was obvious that she was still living with the fears she had written about.

Her husband passed away and she has been living here by herself for quite a while now. Do you suppose she needed to release more of her inner thoughts, or was she merely having a difficult time letting go of her past?

Whatever the case, she looked pitiful crying as she read through her notes. She would pick up a piece of paper that had a name and date on it; as if a birthdate or such, and look up toward the Heavens and close her eyes. She was remembering whoever was on the piece of paper and taking a moment of her time now with them.

Grace was a good-hearted person who always took time for other people. She always seemed to put what she wanted off to the side so she could help another person out.

She was not greedy in the least, with her time, money, wisdom, or any other aspect about her. She certainly was one of a kind for sure. She was someone who I would have picked to be my mother, but I thank God for the one I was given; even if she didn't appear to be very motherly at times. I understood, really I did.

I was just glad to be a part of Grace's life and now she was opening up her past to me as well. What a great thing for me to be a part of; I was learning how to be a friend and I had the best teacher for the job too.

Chapter Three

As we were going through the box of Grace's past, I was intrigued to see how many poems she had written. Each poem had a meaning and each poem had a place in her heart. She could recall an event or time in her life for each piece of paper in the overstuffed shoebox. She had poems written as prayers, poems written for her friends and family who had passed away, and poems for life events over her years.

It was interesting to read through and watch as her story almost came to life through her words. The poem grace had written *"Pick Up Your Faith In Each Other"* sheds a completely new light on the way people should act toward one another.

If only my life was as easy as writing a poem to portray how I was feeling or to bring the *inner me* out. I had to write stories; some long and some short, but felt the need to get everything out all at once. The poems Grace had been writing were of her life in bits and pieces.

Pick Up Your Faith In Each Other
Hold on tight to your loved ones
Kiss them every night
Tell them that you love them
And everything will be alright

Pick up your faith in each other
Build a bond as strong as nails
Keep your faith in Jesus
His absolute love prevails

Share your dreams of tomorrow
Built upon your children's love
Keep faith in each other
and our heavenly Father up above

Bend on your knees and pray
Tell Him what you fear
Hang tight onto His love
His guidance will persevere

Keep faith in tomorrow
Share your hopes and dreams today
Keep your faith in Jesus
And wash your fears away

Share your dreams of tomorrow
Built upon your children's love
Keep faith in each other
and our heavenly Father up above

Pick up your faith in each other
Build a bond as strong as nails
Keep your faith in Jesus
His absolute love prevails

My life was still in its early stages and I was too young to appreciate what it took for Grace to share what she knew. Granted she was older than I was, but we were still pretty good friends too.

I could never imagine what Grace had endured throughout her life. She had spent more time alive and learning than anyone I knew. She was born in the 20th century and had been alive when President number thirty-seven was in office. She had lived through some of the worst headliners known such as the school shootings, the terror attacks on September 11th, the Gulf War, the war in Afghanistan, the war on terror, and was still seeing life events that she was writing about.

She lived through segregation of blacks and whites being born and raised in North Carolina. She experienced the fate of being paddled in school; no one does that anymore, parents aren't even allowed to legally punish their own children without fear of going to jail for child abuse.

No wonder this box had all of these little jotted notes from her past; she had experienced so much that this was the only way she could keep up with her own world.

*****

As Sarah and I worked our way through the shoebox and shared the memories it contained, I showed her the poem I had written for the Sandy Hook elementary school shooting that happened in Newtown, Connecticut, on December 14, 2012. The poem called, "*We Need Your Heart*" that I had written to help me deal with the emotional torment that I felt just imaging the sheer terror those children and teachers felt that day.

We Need Your Heart
Heavenly Father up above
Your world below needs your love
We are finding it hard to trust
Please come place your hand on us

Neighbors are killing
Children's blood is spilling
Misfortune is all around
Hate is becoming abound

Were only sinners and believers
Trying to understand
We live day to day
Holding onto your hand

We need a place to start
We need your heart
Fear lingers through our mind

Don't you think it's time
We need your heart

Smile down on us
Bring us together once again
Help me love thy neighbor
Let me be their friend

Put your hand down on us
Light us with your smile
Guide us with your mercy
We ask you as your child

Were only sinners and believers
Trying to understand
We live day to day
Holding onto your hand

We need a place to start
We need your heart
Fear lingers through our mind
Don't you think it's time
We need your heart

Sarah wiped away her tears and read the poem once more before handing it back to me. Her poor little nose was swollen and red from crying. Her cheeks were rosy too. This innocent girl was being exposed to the same feelings I had written that fateful day.

I excused myself and went to get my Bible placed so carefully on my nightstand. As I was walking back into the room, Sarah looked at me with tears rolling down over her rosy red cheeks and handed me another poem I had written called, *"Feeling The Pain Once More"* and stood up out of her seat. She walked over to the doorway and sucked in a big breath of fresh air, and wiped her nose on the tissue she retrieved from her pocket.

As I glanced down at the poem she handed me, I realized it was the poem I had written for my brother who committed suicide when he was very young.

Feeling The Pain Once More
You left this world to early
Suicide was your escape
Fear and rage pour from us now
As we try to respond to the hate

No reason, no remorse
Trying to answer why
There was no reason for this pain
No reason for you to die

Your passing was a tragedy
One of great misfortune
Reliving the past
Reliving the torture

Tears and hate are common now
Feeling the pain once more
Your death was quick and relentless
You became a memory forever more

Struggling for the answers
Trying to brighten a light
Facing life without you
Crying night after night

We will meet again one day
This in fact I am sure
I want to learn the reason why
Was there ever a cure

I will always remember you
No matter how many years pass
You were my brother, my friend
More than a memory from my past

I recall the day I found him as if it were yesterday. He looked so helpless setting in the car with the gun still in his hand. His lifeless face with eyes bright and blue staring out the window. Feeling the pain of such a tragedy, I too walked over to the doorway to get a fresh breath of air.

*****

"Grace, why did your brother commit suicide? Do you even know? Was his life so tortuous to him that he felt that was the only way he had out of whatever his problems were?" I hated to be so intrusive with my questions, but could not resolve the feelings I had when it dawned on me that one of my own brothers could do the same.

I made the decision at that time to watch my brothers and sisters closely for signs of their struggle. I needed to open myself up more to my family and stop being so reclusive too. I needed to be a part of my family and not just another helpless kid in need of a bright future.

Maybe that was Grace's plan for me today. Was she opening herself up to me so I could see what I needed to do with my own life? Was she trying to be a silent teacher and guide me to a life of hope and love?

I needed to see past my own negativity and focus on the world that was revolving around me. Maybe I needed to pay forward to others what I had been taught.

Recalling Grace's poem called *"Smile Down On Us Jesus"* gave me the strength I think I needed to make me see that I needed to change, but not just for me either. I needed the world to know that I was here and they needed to know who I was. But who was I? I was a writer and in my own eyes; the best writer ever. I needed the world to see this too.

I needed to help Grace's poems be seen by the world so they could have the same impact on others. I needed to pay forward what Grace was teaching me today; how to just be myself, how to just be me.

Smile Down On Us Jesus
Life is getting harder
More people feeling pain
Tears fall down more easily
Pouring like the rain

Smiles have gone away
Replaced by grim and fear
Love thy neighbor they say
Take me by the hand and pray

Smile down on us Jesus
Wrap us in your arms
Keep us safe and warm tonight
Keep us free from harm

We pray for family and friends
Our faith will never end
Smile down on us Jesus
Wrap us in your arms
Keep us safe and warm tonight
Keep us free from harm

War and hate fill the street
Gloom and despair fill the air
We all need faith in Jesus
We all have one moment to spare

Hug your loved ones daily

Kiss them on the cheek
Smile at a stranger and
Build faith among the weak

Smile down on us Jesus
Wrap us in your arms
Keep us safe and warm tonight
Keep us free from harm

We pray for family and friends
Our faith will never end
Smile down on us Jesus
Wrap us in your arms
Keep us safe and warm tonight
Keep us free from harm

I really wanted the world to see what Grace had been sharing with me and I also really wanted Grace to continue showing me what she spent her life writing about. As I turned to go back into the room where Grace was, I saw her open the Bible that she was holding and trace her fingertips across the page in front of her.

She was crying and the tears were freely flowing down her cheeks now. She sat there staring at the pages and her face held the expression of a love lost or a memory too good to let go. When I asked Grace if she was okay, her reply to me was "yes, I am just thinking. I wrote another poem about asking God for guidance, and I wonder what ever happened to it."

I fumbled around through the shoebox and stopped briefly to glance at some of the tidbits of handwritten memories on the papers inside. I learned of her friends she had and family that were gone now and a feeling came over me as if I had known these people all of my life.

I felt like I belonged here with Grace today, as if the souls of those who had passed away pulled me into Grace's world for a purpose. I was helping Grace live by reliving her past with her and it felt wonderful. I finally felt like I belonged somewhere and that I had a purpose.

Reading the little notes on each piece of paper reminded me of my own family; how *"apart"* we all seemed to have become over the years. I really didn't know my mother; just like Grace didn't get to know hers. I barely saw my father; just like Grace barely knew hers. I saw most of my brothers and sisters each day, but I wondered how much I really *knew* them. What if something bad were to happen, would they all know how much I love them? What if another terror attack was to occur; would they all become one and help each other? What if something terrible happened to my family; God forbid, I hope nothing bad ever happens to anyone I know, but if something bad ever did happen would they know how I felt about them?

I found a poem titled, *"I Rely On You To Guide Me"* and I asked Grace if that was the poem she was referring to. She nodded her head and I handed her the poem.

I Rely On You To Guide Me
I rely on you to guide me
As I walk through life each day
Holding on tight to your words
Confessing as I pray

I smile up to the heavens
Wishing I could see your face
The sun shines and gives me hope
That comforts my mind with your grace

The birds sing and the wind blows soft
the whispers of your words fill my mind

as I kneel by my bed each night to pray
the meaning of your love starts to shine

I am grateful to you for all that you are
The love and guidance you provide to me
Sharing your gospel with your children below
Heavenly father are you hearing me

I rely on you to guide me
As I walk through life each day
Holding on tight to your words
Confessing as I pray

I smile up to the heavens
Wishing I could see your face
The sun shines and gives me hope
That comforts my mind with your grace

As Grace sat there reading the poem to herself, I realized that I needed to have some guidance in my life too and reached out to take hold of Grace's hand. "Grace, I want you to know how much you mean to me. You have been the best friend I could ever ask for and I thank you for that. I am glad that we have had today to learn more about each other and I wouldn't trade this for all the world. You have made me realize that I need to be a better person and that I too have a purpose in life. My words that I write were meant to be seen by everyone and I will do my very best to make that happen. I want to do a favor for you and if it is ok, I would like to help you get a few of your poems published. I know that you may think that is kind of silly, but I really like each one of them, and they have helped me see that I need to change who I am."

*****

I tried to smile as I reached over the table to hug Sarah. "Thank you for thinking my poems are worthy of

29

being published, but I just don't feel comfortable sharing them with the world. They are *my* memories and *my* feelings. They helped me heal through life when I had no one there other than a piece of paper and a pen."

I thumbed through each piece of paper still inside the box, not really sure what I was looking for. I found little love notes that Mel and I had written back and forth, and notes from my brother before he died. I found birth dates of people who had had passed on already and seeing each of those tugged at my heart a little bit more. The memories were flooding through me and I was becoming overwhelmed with reliving my past all over again.

I couldn't help but wonder why Sarah thought it would be a good idea to show my poems to anyone. Why would anyone even care; I was a nobody and nobody's are just that...nobody.

I hoped that Sarah learned why I showed these things to her today. She needed to open up to her family a bit and let the world see what I saw in her. She was a bright child with an enormous future ahead of her. She was living in a shell and was not seeing the world around her, including her own family.

Sarah needed to know her mother and father on a more personal level, not just that they were alive and sharing the same home with her. She needed to know them better than I knew my parents. Her brothers and sisters were all happy children who lived their life different from Sarah. They had friends and hobbies they shared daily with each other, and were not closed in to their own little world.

Sarah was full of life and showed this in her writing. She was stubborn enough to make sure each *"i"* was dotted and each *"t"* was crossed, making her work very neat and presentable. She was a happy child who had an interest in life, but never showed this side of herself to anyone. She liked the comfort of being a *"nobody"* too.

As I sat there thinking of how much more I could do for Sarah, I had decided that maybe having a poem or two, but no more than that, published might be okay. What did I really have to lose?

If Sarah felt confident enough in the words I had written throughout my life to show the world, who was I to stand in her way? I made the decision to let her pick one or two poems that she felt would be the best to show. I didn't really care if they won a blue ribbon at the fair, but if they helped someone heal from a tragedy in their life, then my words served their purpose. They helped me heal time and time again, so maybe others could benefit in that way too.

"Sarah, if you could pick one or two of my poems to publish, which would you pick? I guess if it helps someone, then I will allow you to take a copy of a couple and do what you can with them."

*****

I looked up at grace for the first time with a smile on my face. "Are you serious Grace, you will let me put your poems in print? Grace nodded her head and smiled back at me.

I wasn't sure which poems to pick they were all so touching. I liked the poem written for the Sandy Hook children, but I also liked the ones she had written for her husband. This was going to be a tough pick.

Chapter Four

I was still digging around in the box glancing at each item in there when I came across another poem that Grace had written for her husband, *"Only Me And Only You"* and couldn't help but read it word for word.

Only Me And Only You.

The blue in your eyes
The love in your heart
The smile upon your face
You had me from the start

The years have shown a great life
For me to be by your side
Sharing my life with you
And being your loving bride.

Age is upon us now
Wrinkles are on my face.
Your eyes still shine with love
Showing your presence and grace.

Taking the time to make a memory
Sharing life's ups and downs
Waking with you each morning
You holding me in your arms.

I dread the day you leave this earth
Never more to wake with you
Never more to see your face.
Always remember how much I love you.

Take the time to share with me
The love we always knew
Walk with me through life's dream

Only me and only you.

I give to you my everything
My hope, my dreams, and my love
I only want what's best for you
You gave me more than I could dream of

Always remember what we've shared
Remember our memories too
No one could love me ever again
My heart holds only room for you.

Take the time to share with me
The love we always knew
Walk with me through life's dream
Only me and only you.

Grace so elegantly wrote these words for the man she loved so dearly. It was a tragedy that he was no longer here sharing the world with her. It was obvious that she loved him and the words she wrote were a testament to this.

As the day was coming to an end and it was starting to get darker outside, I realized that the entire day had been spent with Grace. I learned so much from sharing in her memories that I wanted to make life a better place for her now. I wanted to make my life better now too.

I didn't want to live in fear of wondering "*what-if*" another terror attack happened again or "*what-if*" someone goes on another shooting rampage. I wanted to just "*live*" and I was able to do that now. Grace had shown me how to live. I didn't have to be afraid of life anymore. I didn't have to be a recluse.

Grace was picking up the papers to place back into her shoebox and she finally had a smile on her face once more. Seeing Grace like this made me wonder if this was as healing for her as it was for me.

She had a reason for sharing her shoebox with me; I just knew it. I couldn't help but wonder if the reason were to teach me how to be a better writer and live more vicariously through the words I had written.

I wanted to do something for Grace to show my gratitude for the interview and for her sharing all of her life with me that she kept tucked in her box of memories.

I decided that I was going to pick two of Grace's poems and make sure they reached people everywhere. Others would have the ability to heal by reading her words. Even though they were written at a time of Grace's life were torment and heartbreak were prevalent, they were sure to help someone else experiencing the same feelings.

If they saved one life, if they helped one grieving person, if they helped a parent, if they helped anyone at all then Grace's words would transpire to be worthy. Grace was not just a "*nobody*" as she called herself; Grace was a "*somebody*" and more importantly, she was my friend.

Realizing I still had pieces of paper in my hand that I had not looked through yet, I opened each one and read names and more dates, more anniversaries, notes from her husband Mel. There was another poem tucked inside newspaper articles from various dates that mentioned taking prayer out of our everyday life and making it illegal in most places to pray.

The poem was written to show that prayer needed to be brought back, to be reborn again in everyone's life. Prayer was needed in the world to help prevent failure, to show respect for a Higher being, to help people realize why they were here in the first place.

Keeping people from having nativity scenes in their front yard or at a courthouse was not the answer that people needed. There were a handful of naysayers looking to create fear in others and removing our Lord and Savior was the only thing they could think of to make their point known.

The poem titled, *"I Try To Keep My Faith In You"* was written to show Grace's support in spreading the word of God. She wanted every home to have a Bible and every home to say their prayers before closing their eyes at night.

I Try To Keep My Faith In You

Looking up into the heavens
I wonder where you are
you are needed more now than ever
both here at home and afar

Tragedy and mourning
Both building with despair
Love and hope lie carelessly
Losing faith, hope and prayer

Why were you absent
Where have you been
Why all the destruction
Will it ever end

I try to keep my faith in you
Praying night and day
Wishing you could take the pain
And make the misery go away

My tears flow freely now
My faith in you still there
Trying to hang onto your words
Wishing you could hear my prayers

Why were you absent
Where have you been
Why all the destruction
Will it ever end

I try to keep my faith in you
Praying night and day
Wishing you could take the pain
And make the misery go away

I knew that Grace was a good person and I also knew that she wrote these words to show her love and support for others; not just herself. She was looking out for her fellow people and yet she had kept it all tucked inside her shoebox.

"Grace, I will pick two of your poems to take for publishing, but will you do me the favor of signing your name to the bottom of the copy I make. I want to keep these as my own treasures and start a shoebox of my own." I knew that today was going to be a good day, but I really had no idea how good.

I learned about Grace inside and out. I learned that she saw more than her fair share of pain in her lifetime. I learned that she was spiritual in her way of life even more than I knew before. I learned that she felt pain every day, but I never saw that until today.

*****

Grace stopped what she was doing and sat down beside Sarah at the table. "Sarah, I will gladly sign the poems for you, but I want you to do me one favor." Sarah nodded her head and listened carefully to me speak.

"I want you to show your shoebox of memories to people who mean more to you than life itself; your mom, your dad, your brothers and sisters, everyone who needs to know how you feel about them. My biggest regret was not ever showing or sharing my memories to anyone before you. My husband saw a few things in my collection, but very little. I didn't think he cared to see what I was keeping. Little did I know that he would have loved seeing all the little notes, the poems, and other tidbits written on each piece of paper."

I took ahold of Sarah's hand and said, "You have a special gift in you Sarah. A gift of life that can be shared to others in a way like no other. You care about people, but you just have a little trouble showing the real you. I want you to show the world who you are…inside and out. I want them to see in you what I see in you."

Sarah reached across the table to hug me and she was crying. "Child, there is no need to shed tears over me. I only want what is best for you and that would be to share your writing. Make yourself a *"somebody"* in this world filled with people who are afraid to show who they really are."

I knew the impact on this young girl was overwhelming, but I also knew that she was the type of person who could make something of herself with a little encouragement.

"I want you to continue writing and show the world who you are. I want you to keep getting good grades in school. I want you to love your family and let them know this. I want you to reach for the stars knowing you can take hold of the moon too if you wish."

Sarah stopped crying long enough to look at me and say, "Thank you for today Grace, it has helped me realize who I want to be in life. I want to be just like you." Hearing these words made my heart smile and I was happy that Sarah saw through my tears to understand why today's interview was as important to me as it was to her.

*****

I couldn't help but wonder how Grace kept all of her memories from everyone she knew for so long. She was not really the type of person not to speak her mind or let others know what she was thinking. She loved life and people, so keeping these a secret was not something I figured she would do.

Either way, I had to pick two of her poems to take to my publisher that I had been sending my articles too.

My publisher was one of the best and I knew she was bound to like Grace's poems too. I wondered if my publisher wanted to publish an article about Grace after the interview today. It sure couldn't hurt to ask and see if it was a good idea.

As I glanced through Grace's poems trying to pick only two; I found that it was rather hard to pick from any of them. I wanted all of them and knew that Grace was not going to go for that.

I like the last poem trying to keep faith in God when it was not politically correct. Why did people have to be so arrogant and what made them think the world needed to follow their way of life anyway. Just because they didn't believe gave them no reason to take something from those who did believe. Where were the rights of the believer's?

I liked the poem written for the students at Sandy Hook too. The words were a reflection of how much God's presence was needed. If prayer hadn't been taken out of schools, maybe this would have never happened. If praying anywhere hadn't been turned into something shameful maybe the world would be a better place all around.

The more I thought about the background of why the poems were written to begin with, the more furious I became over losing my rights to be able to worship my Savior. What gives anyone the right to tell me when I can talk to my God? What gives anyone the right to interfere with anything between God and me? No one had that right, no one!

I could see why Grace was so unwilling to share these poems with the world. She would have been dragged to the center of town and tarred, feather, and publically chastised in front of everyone who really wanted to say something, but feared the outcome of their words. Was Grace looking at me as someone who was not afraid to speak, even if it was written words? I had to do this now; I was determined to see this through.

I knew that it was not right for me to force my God onto others, share Him yes, talk about Him yes, but force Him, no. I knew that there were people had different ways of thinking and didn't want anything to do with religion, for whatever reason. Some were ashamed, some confused, some embarrassed, and some just didn't know so they followed the path of others rather than taking their own road.

For whatever reason there was always going to be someone who had something negative to say about worshipping their Savior. There was always going to be that person who said they didn't want to have anything to do with God, theirs or anyone else's. There was always going to be good and bad with people, no matter what walk of life they came from.

I understood the task put in front of me and I knew that it was something I had to do. Grace had opened this window of opportunity for me and I had to run with it. I also knew that there was going to be a problem with bringing religious beliefs to the forefront, even if it was written in words.

There were people who were not going to like hearing that people who believed had rights too. There were people who did not want to hear about God or read his scripture. There were people who did not want to say prayer in school or see religious sculpture displayed publically. There were also people who would do whatever they could to stop those who wanted nothing more than to share their God with everyone.

I kept jotting down notes to myself to remember to ask my publisher when I spoke with her next. I wanted to know how controversial this would become and how much it was going to affect the people who wanted to be able to recognize they had rights too.

I had to do this right and be careful how I handled each written word to make sure no one was offended. I was not attempting to hurt, force, belittle, shame, or even degrade those who didn't want to have a relationship with their Savior. They had that choice to make on their own. I wanted to help those who did want to have a relationship with their God and not punished for doing so.

Each side had rights – those that wanted the relationship with the Lord and those that wanted nothing to do with Him at all. Everyone has that choice and I knew this.

What bothered me was being forced not to be able to have my relationship in the same way as those who wanted nothing to do with Him.

*****

I knew that Sarah understood the path in front of her now that our interview had completed. She was a bright girl and knew that this was a task only she would accept. She had the ability to put into words what others only thought, and this made her an exception to the rule.

Sarah would be able to help the readers of her stories go places that only she could point them towards. She was the only one who could tell the story in a way to reflect the path that she had taken to get where she was in life too.

Her direction was now pointed toward life, love, and doing onto others just as you'd have done onto to you. She finally had a purpose and was able to be a part of society now that she knew where she was going.

I imagined how Sarah was going to react and rightfully so. She accepted this task graciously and set out to pick two of my poems to bring with her. Now, I could have shared more than two and I more than likely will, but I need to make sure she can handle being a *"somebody"* first. I knew my poems had powerful words in them and I also knew that Sarah could portray just how thankful life can be through written or now even spoken words.

I was grateful to Sarah for wanting to interview me and I was even more grateful that she opened up her own hidden side during the process. She was not as different as everyone assumed she was, she just kept to herself to avoid the pain of being hurt. I did the same thing and during these times is when I would write another poem. Sarah was just like me in that regard. She had the ability to write what she felt and others would be able to understand without her actually uttering a word. The word had already been uttered onto paper.

*****

"Grace, I wanted to say thank you one more time for letting me interview you today. I know what I have to do now and I look forward to helping others see who you truly are. You are someone who has been through a lot in your life, but through your faith you have overcome more than just being alive through it all; you lived it."

I glanced back over the poems one more time and selected "*I Struggle With The Words To Say To You*" and "*We Need Your Heart*" knowing that these two poems would portray the words whether written or spoken either way.

The reflection of the life that wrote these words to begin with was an adornment that only God could testify. He made Grace the person she was and I wanted others to see how big a heart He had given her.

Chapter Five

I managed to write a story of my interview with Grace to hand in to Mrs. Bennett. The words flowed freely onto paper as if they were meant to be. I mentioned the events that took place during Grace's life, the struggles she endured, how she overcame devastation, and how she shared with others.

I received an "A" for all of my hard work and appreciated it greatly, but there was something missing from the equation. I needed to be able to speak to my publisher Meg before sending anything in to her. I wanted to prepare her for the material she was going to receive from me and the only way I knew how to do this was write to her so I did:

> *Dear Meg:*
> *I am sharing with you two poems I acquired recently after interviewing my neighbor Grace for extra credit in school. I want you to publish the following story with the two poems as I have written below for you...*

> *Grace...what does this word mean to you? Grace is a name. Grace is a passion. Grace is a feeling that is not easily overcome by fear. Grace is elegance at its finest. Grace is beauty inside and out. More importantly, Grace is a concept taken into your heart when you believe in something or someone enough to share the impression left behind.*
> *Grace to me is a well-defined character of being, a spiritual epitaph of right versus wrong. I recently spent a day with a very dear friend who shared with me her "internal Grace" of the life she lived. The way she shared what was inside of her heart with others was to write poetry. She reflected her many years onto paper for all the*

world to see, but kept each piece in a shoebox covered up in a corner where only she knew they existed.

Grace loved life, she loved her husband, and she loved the Lord. Her Savior was her guiding light; her very presence was a reflection of His being. She felt it overwhelming to be in the glory of Him at her free will until that was all stripped from her. She was not able to share the word of her Lord with others publically. Was she trying to force her love of God onto others? No. Was she spreading gossip of the Bible in a shameful way? No. Was she ashamed to speak the word of her God to others? No. Was she allowed to speak of her God to others without fear? Sadly, no.

The world around her had taken her rights away from her. The right for her to be able to pray when she wanted to and where she wanted to was no longer acceptable. The right for her to display her love for her Lord was ripped from her front lawn every Christmas when she set out her Nativity scene because too many people didn't like seeing it.

Where were her rights as a God-loving woman? She did not have any outside of her own home and Church. She was not able to let her children pray in school or anywhere publically for that matter. There were too many people who felt that it was a right of theirs to pull her rights away from her.

Did Grace have any rights remaining to be able to show others that she loved the Lord? She could, but not publically; it was now against the law. She was no longer able to share His word with fellow parishioners outside of her Church.

What made this wrong? Was being politically correct acceptable even when it meant losing the ability to pray or share prayer with others? Why was it so wrong for prayer to be exposed? Why were so many naysayers able to strip the rights of others away so easily? Where were the rights of those who wanted to worship? Those rights were gone.

The cost of being a religious person was no longer being able to publically share the word of the Lord with others, or share Gospel outside of your Church. It was gone. There were people who did not want to see others in prayer or hear prayer, so the right was taken away from those who wanted to share.

Is there a way to bring the right back to those who so desperately want it back? The only answer is to bring it back as you can, in ways that you can. Grace was living in a time when she was not able to share her God with anyone, no one. This was no longer right, but wrong.

Being religious does not mean that you are being forced to believe what I believe, or even believe in the same God I believe in. Just as long as you believe. My God is my God. Your God is your God. Are they the same? Maybe so, but they sure don't have to be. Do your prayers have to be the same as mine? Not at all. What you say to the Lord is your business and should not be a right taken away from you. No different than having the right to select what you prepare for dinner. Your decisions and choices should not be portrayed as rights that can be stripped from you by another individual. They are yours and yours alone.

Grace wrote poetry to reflect her life and the past she experienced. Please take this opportunity to read through these two poems and see how they impact your life. Then ask yourself if they helped you resolve a problem, or if they made you feel better, maybe they even helped you heal from a situation. Most importantly, realize that the right to speak to your Lord is just that your right.

We Need Your Heart
Heavenly Father up above
Your world below needs your love
We are finding it hard to trust

Please come place your hand on us

Neighbors are killing
Children's blood is spilling
Misfortune is all around
Hate is becoming abound

Were only sinners and believers
Trying to understand
We live day to day
Holding onto your hand

We need a place to start
We need your heart
Fear lingers through our mind
Don't you think it's time
We need your heart

Smile down on us
Bring us together once again
Help me love thy neighbor
Let me be their friend

Put your hand down on us
Light us with your smile
Guide us with your mercy
We ask you as your child

Were only sinners and believers
Trying to understand
We live day to day
Holding onto your hand

We need a place to start
We need your heart
Fear lingers through our mind

Don't you think it's time
We need your heart

I Struggle With The Words To Say To You
Walking in the path of Jesus
Loving life a little more each day
Battling the demons inside me
Trying to wash my sins away

I struggle with the words to say to you
As I kneel in prayer once more
Wishing you could look deep inside me
Counting each tear that hits the floor

Knowing you died for my sins
Gives me hope to fight another day
Wrapping myself in your words
Oh heavenly father hear me pray

The words are trapped in my heart
Their meaning a twisted mess
Listen to the words I say to you
My captive soul wants to confess

Tighter and tighter I cling to you
Holding onto your prayer
Wishing I could walk closer to you
Feeling your love and knowing you care

The days and nights grow shorter for me
Your words are more like song
Confessing my sins to you each day
Knowing your love will keep me strong

I struggle with the words to say to you

46

As I kneel in prayer once more
Wishing you could look deep inside me
Counting each tear that hits the floor

Knowing you died for my sins
Gives me hope to fight another day
Wrapping myself in your words
Oh heavenly father hear me pray

"Nobody" can keep you from being "somebody" in the eyes of the Lord, so reach out to Him and share everything He has to offer you. He is there waiting for you, even if others feel the need to take Him away.

The End

ABOUT THE AUTHOR

"I started writing poems when I was just a little girl. I never did much with anything I wrote other than read it a few times and then put it away. Over the years, everything I had written was lost or destroyed, but the memories I had still lingered on in my mind. We all struggle with things deep within us and outside of us that intrigues our senses enough to want to tell the world about it; why not share what stimulates us and sparks our emotions through a book."

Visit www.tlbliss.com for more information and links to purchase other stories written by TL Bliss.

www.ingramcontent.com/pod-product-compliance
Lightning Source LLC
Chambersburg PA
CBHW071219130626
46555CB00004B/1765